The Day

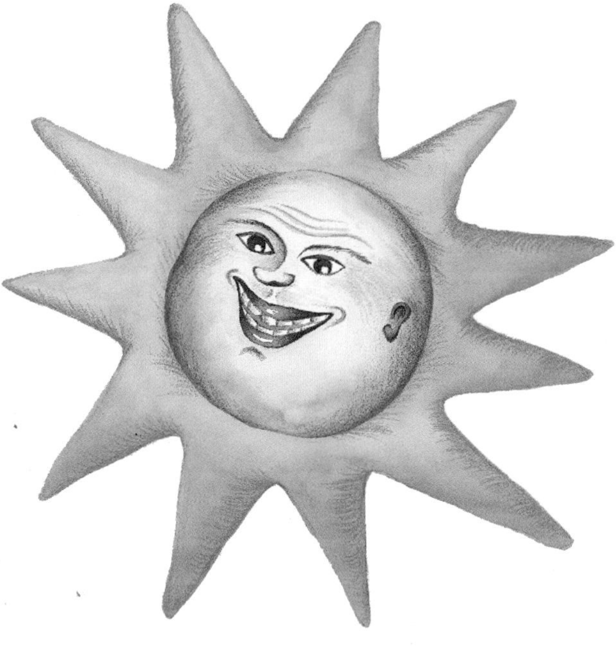

Illustrated by Marie Low

Rigby

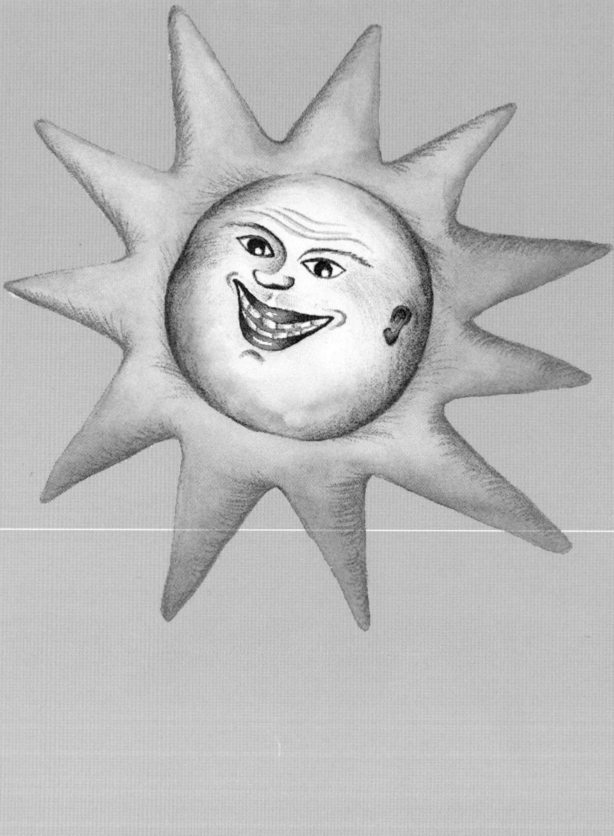

the sun

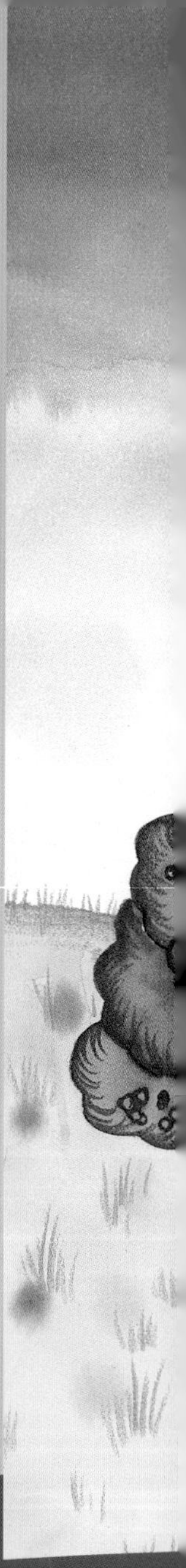

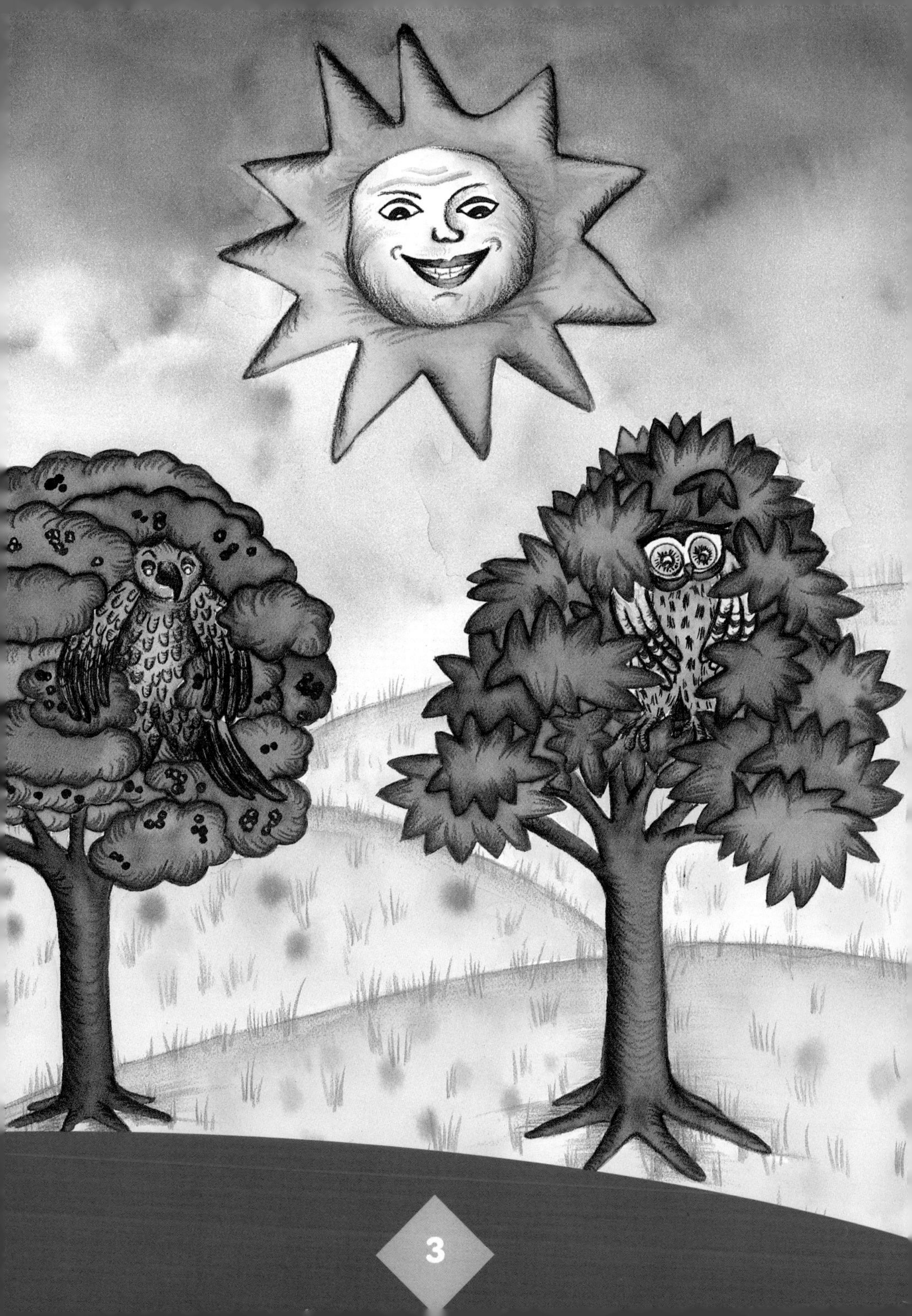

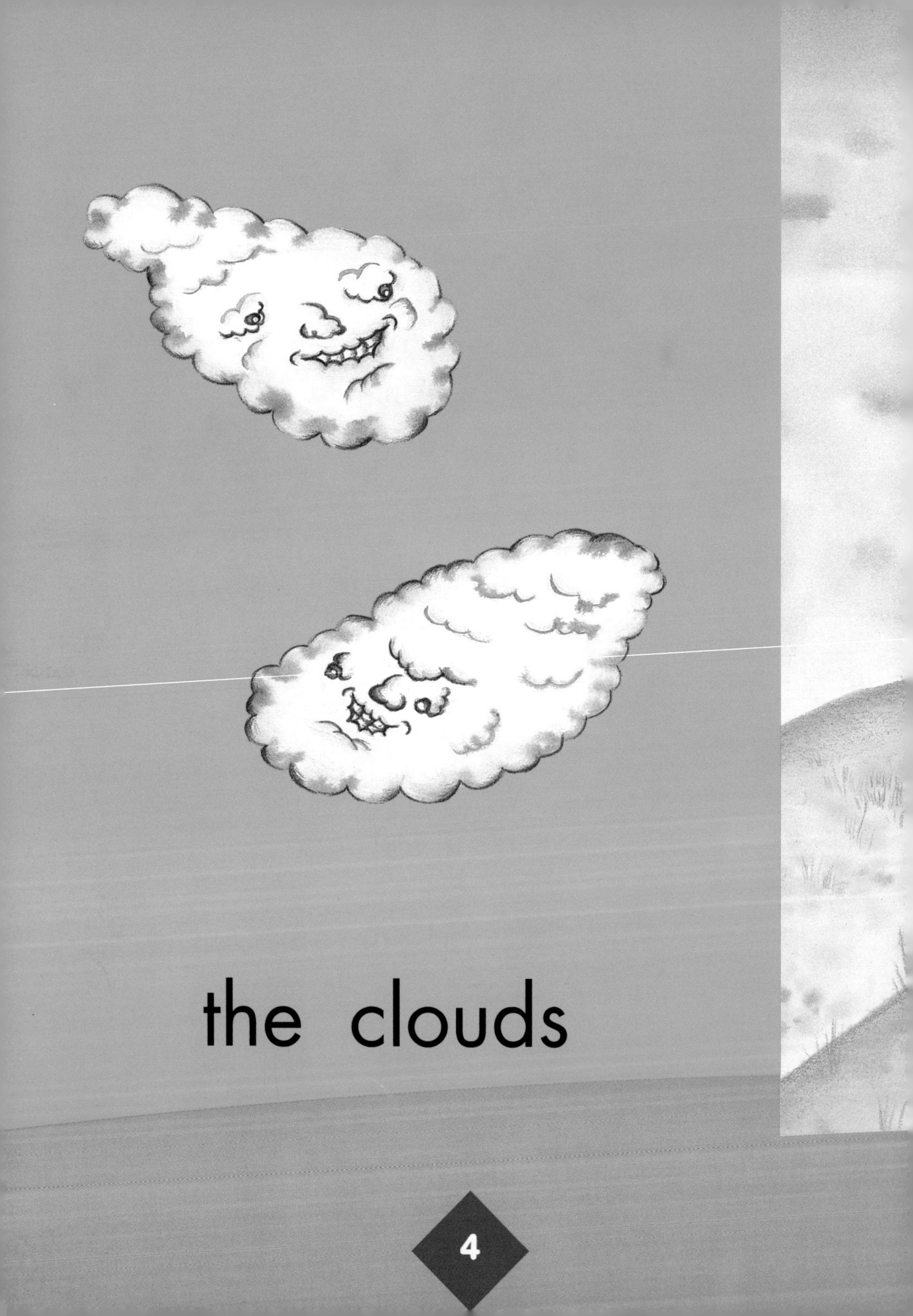

the clouds

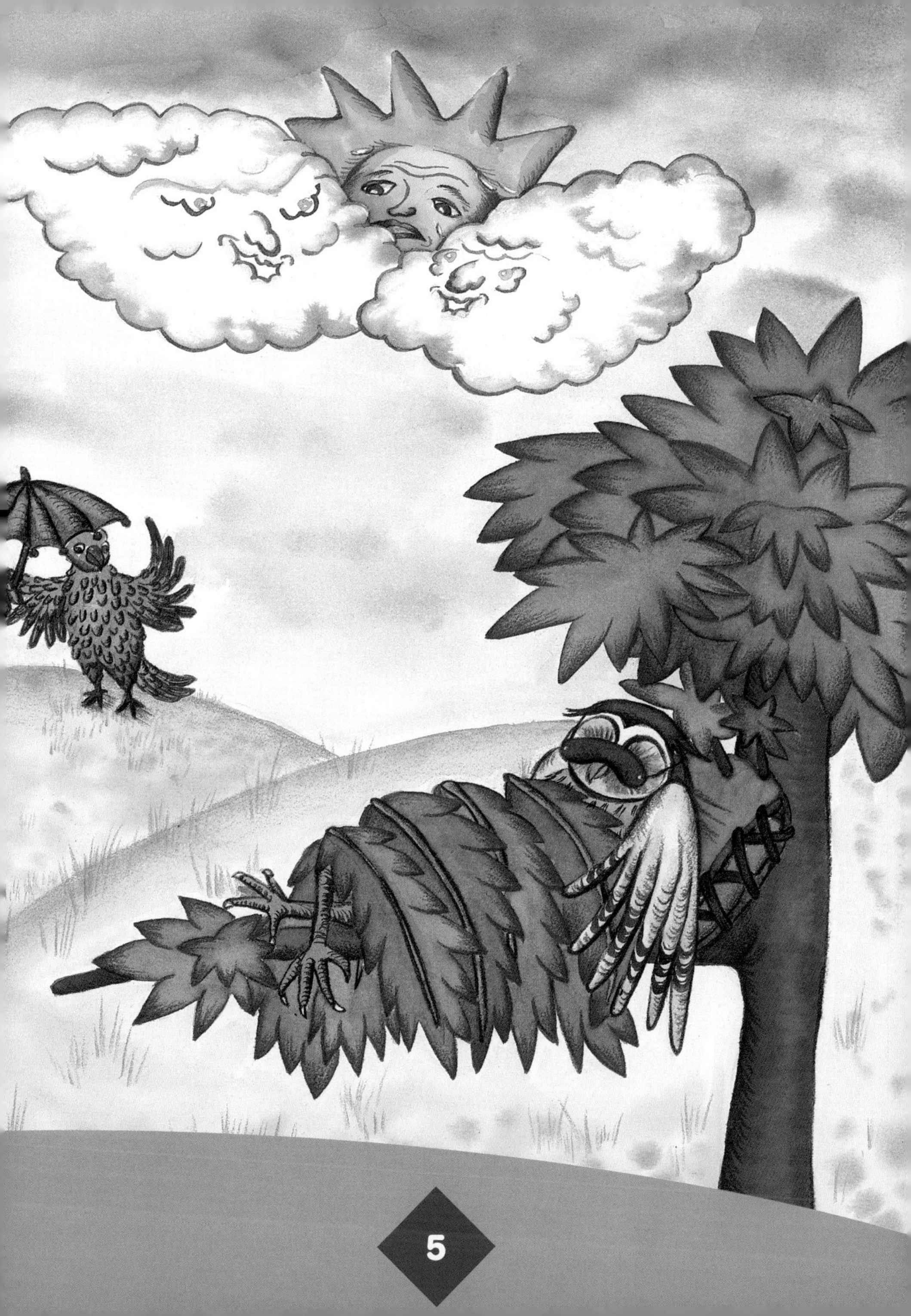

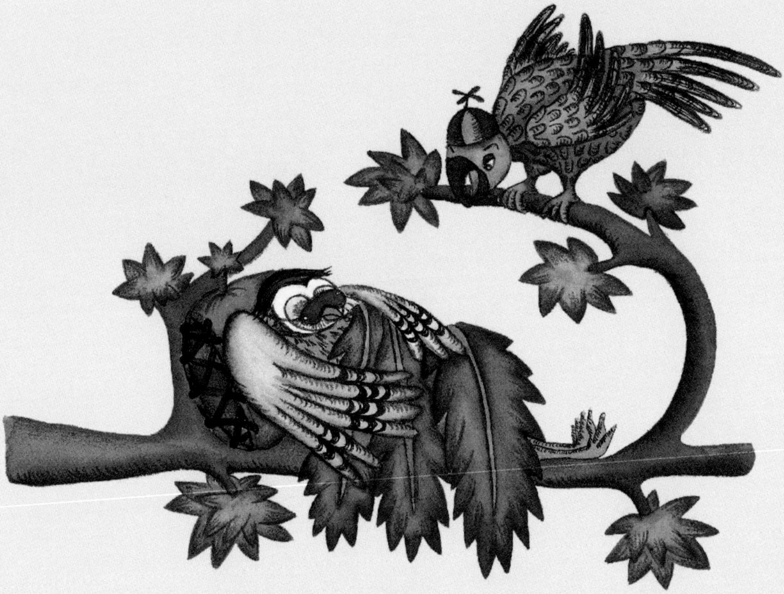

the birds

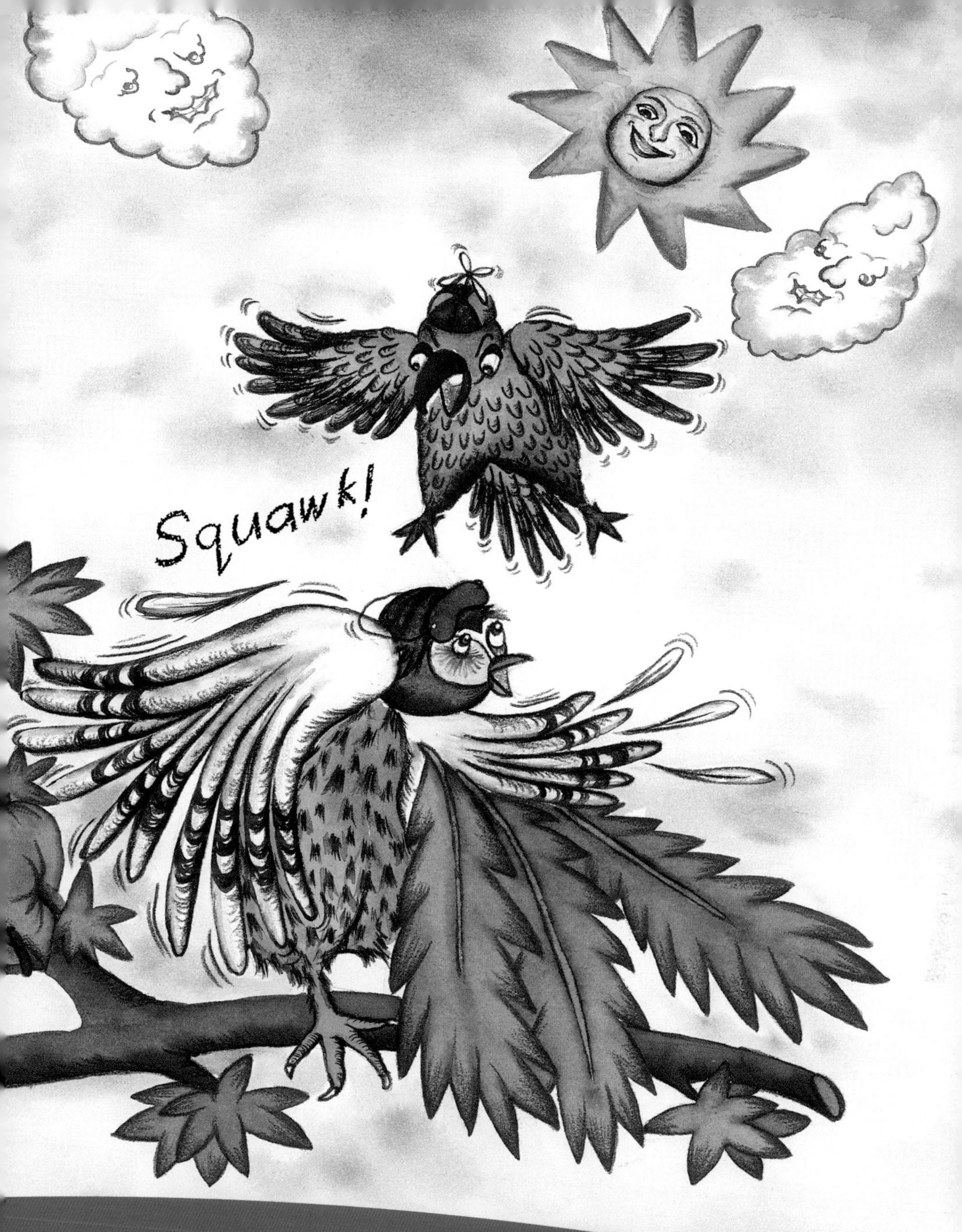
Squawk!

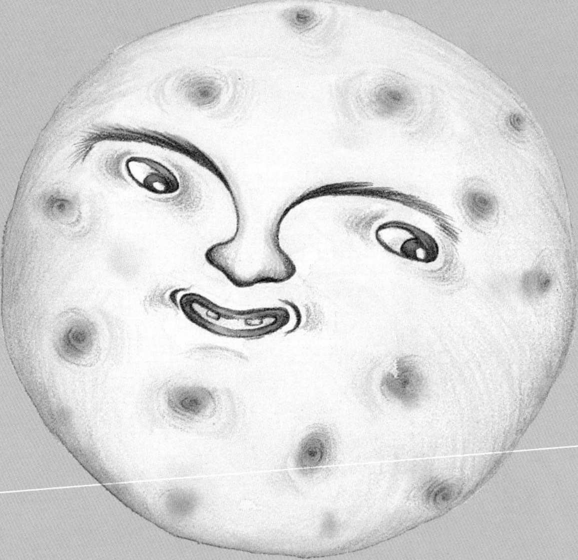

the moon

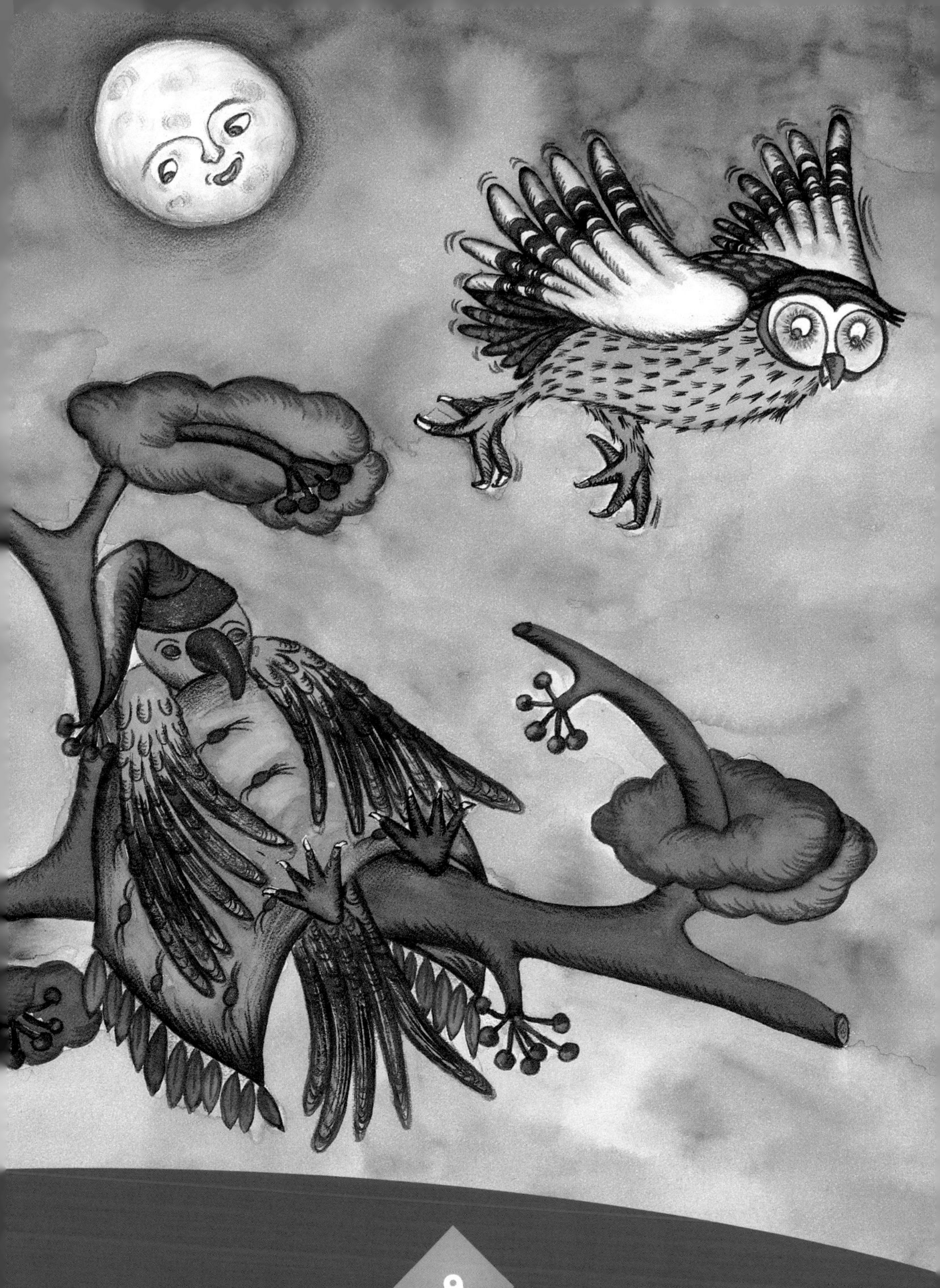

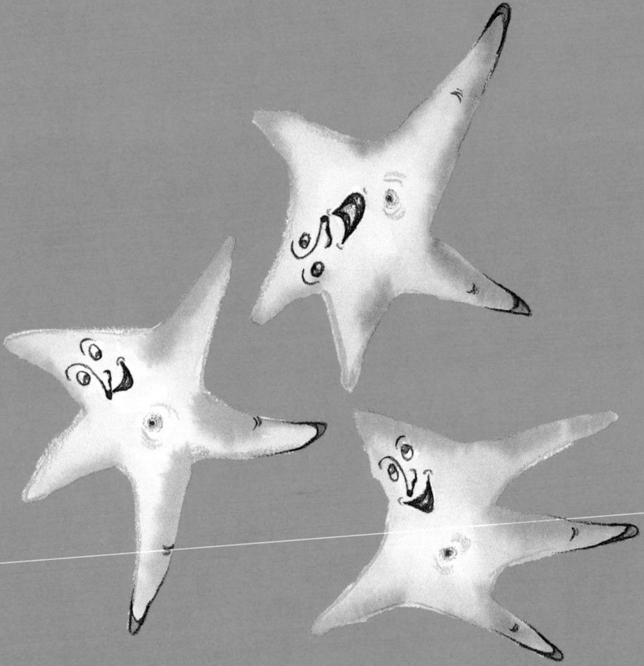

the stars

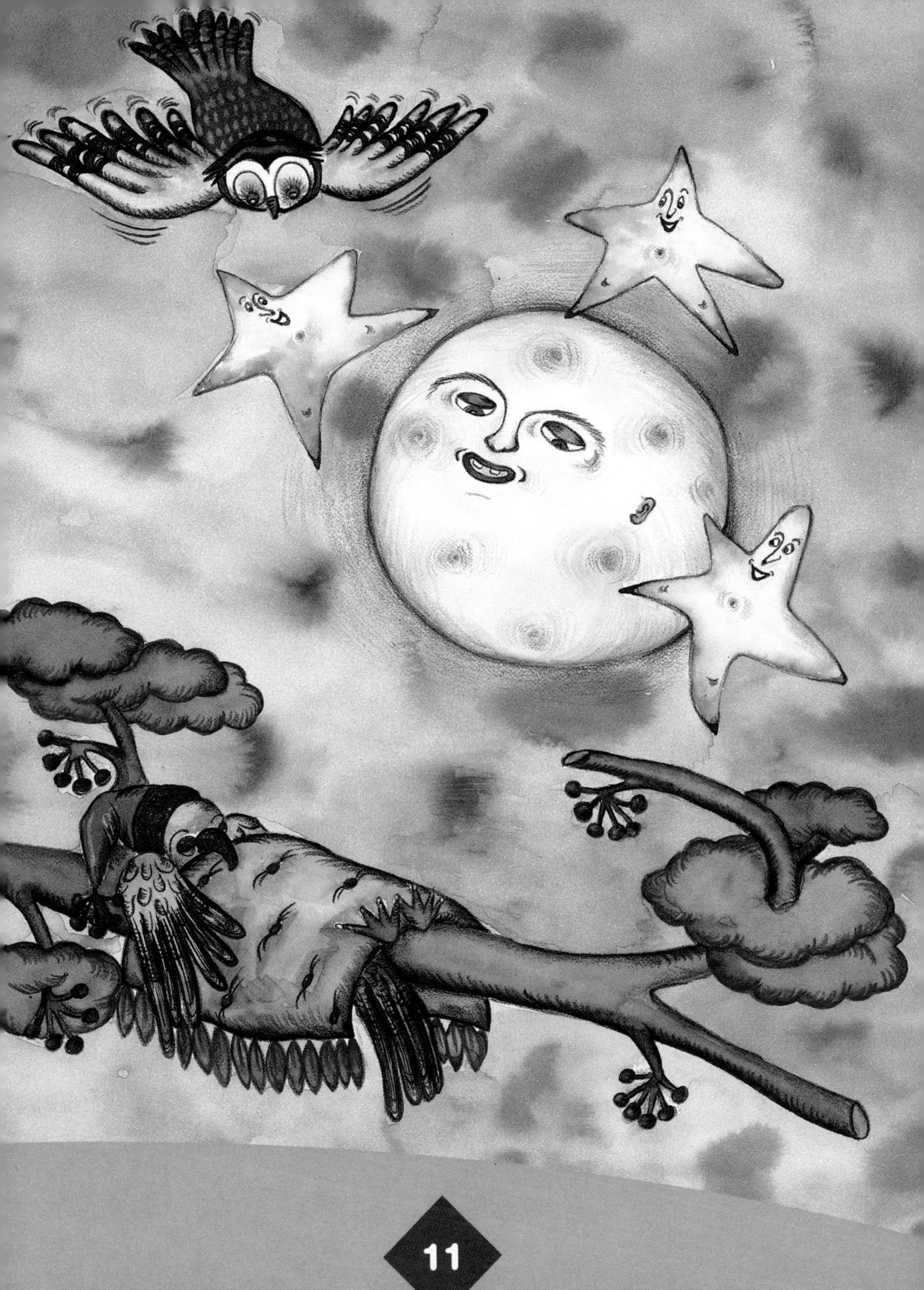

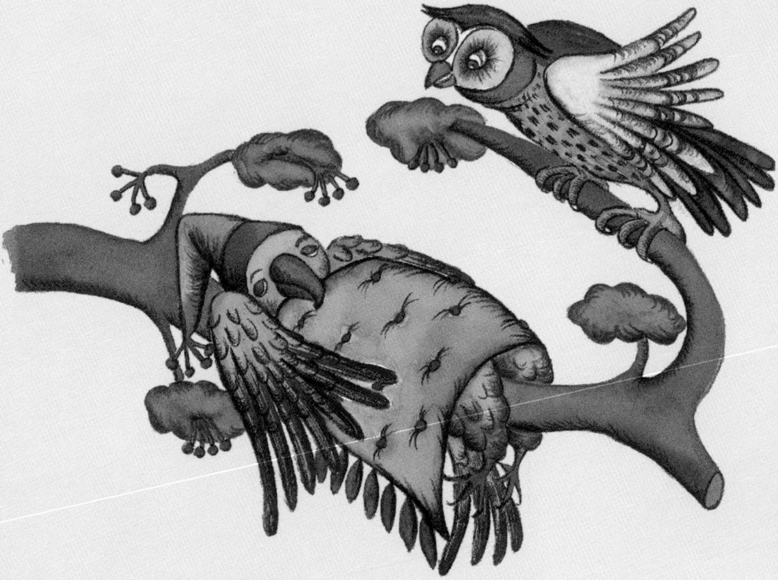

the birds

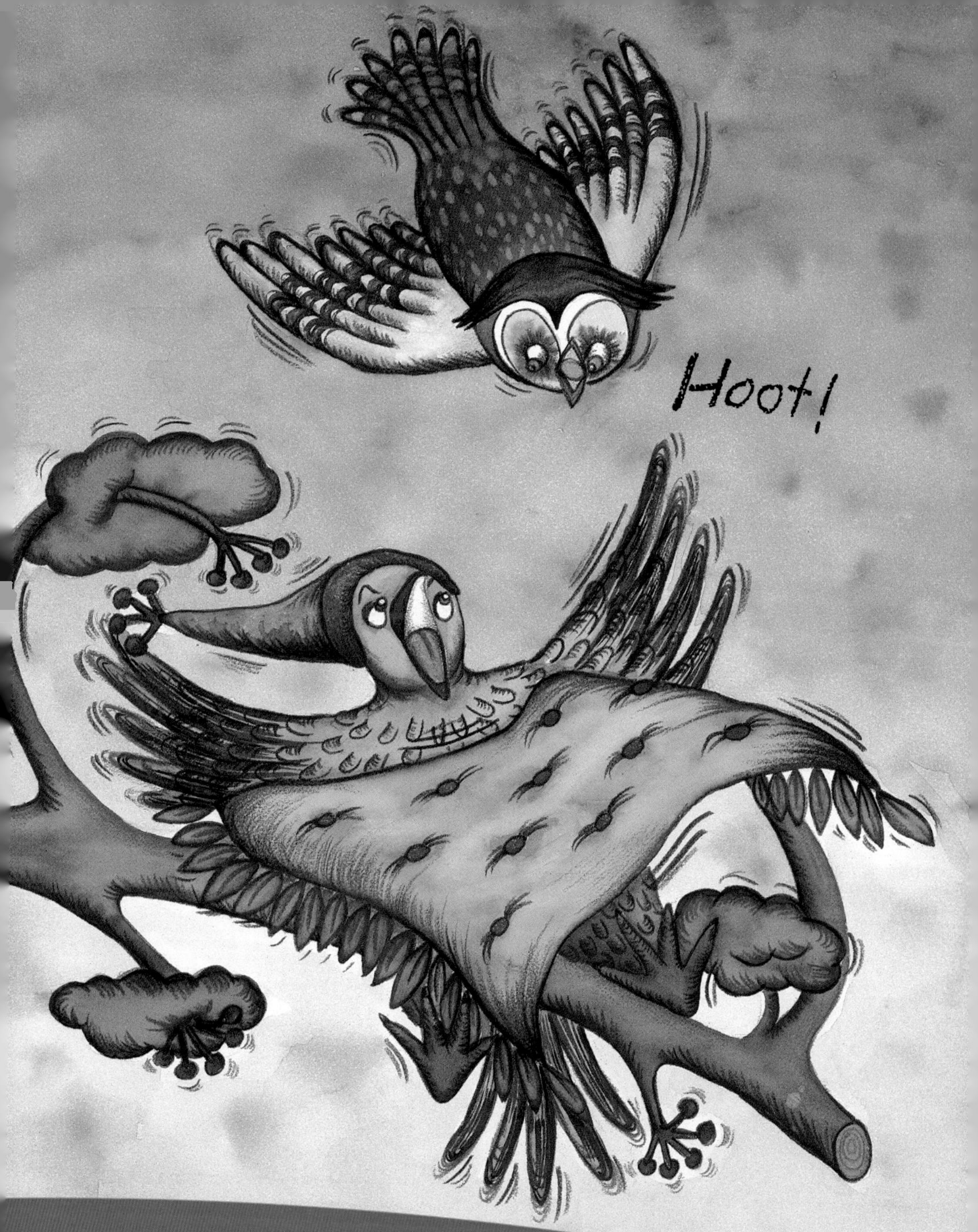
Hoot!

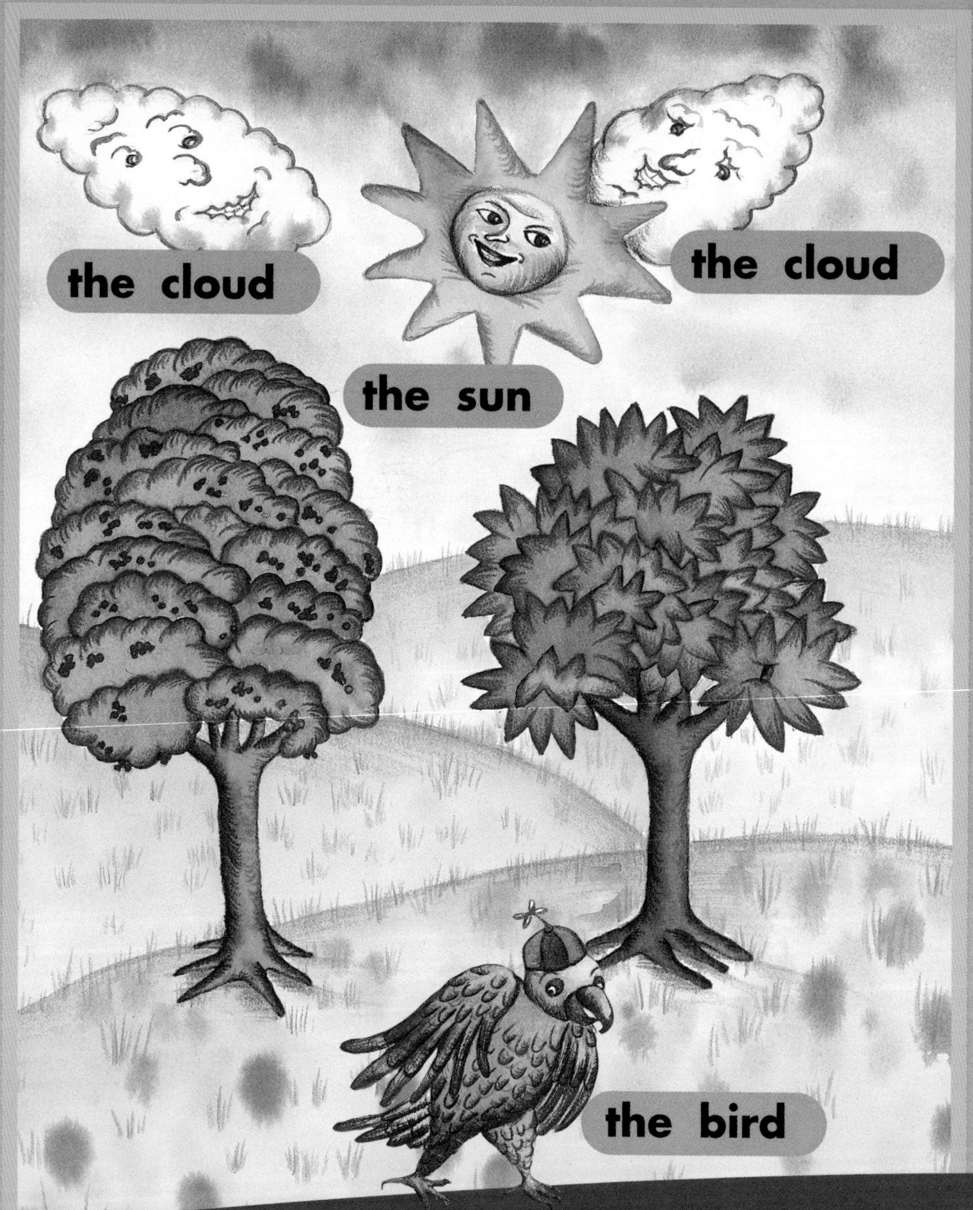
the cloud
the sun
the cloud
the bird

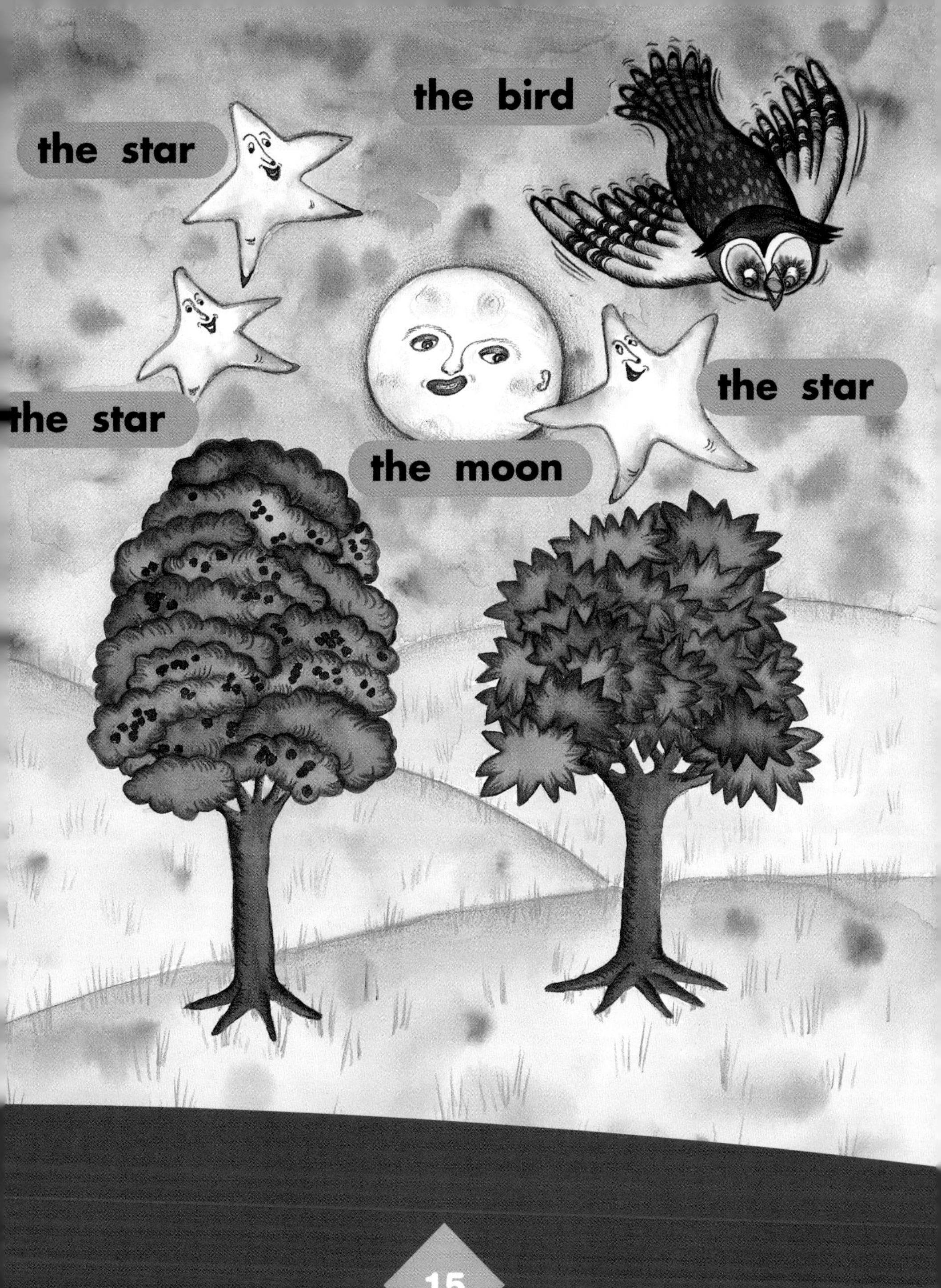
the bird
the star
the star
the star
the moon

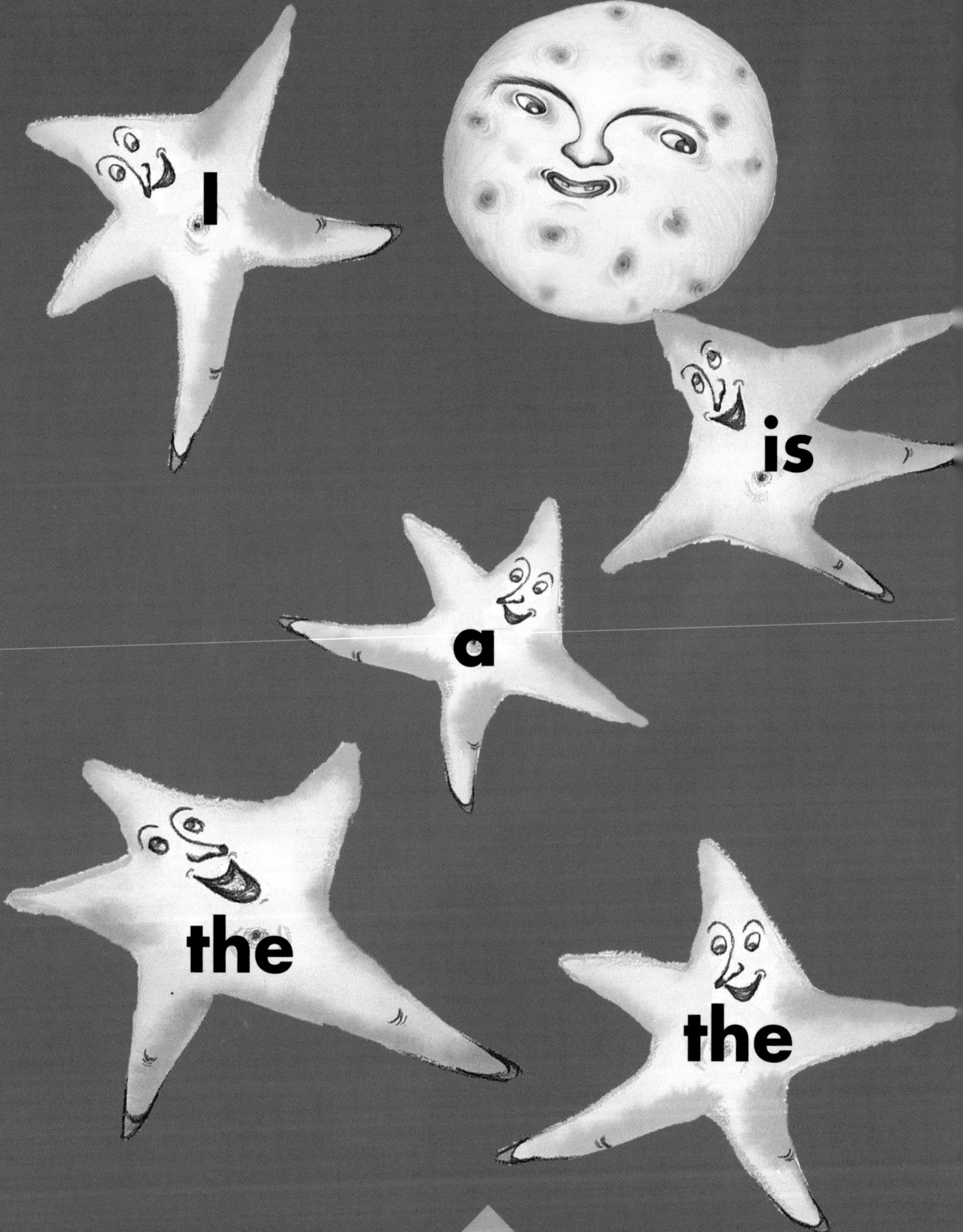
I
is
a
the
the